To William TC
For Sandie and Paul PH

First American edition 1994 published by Orchard Books
First published in Great Britain by ABC, All Books for Children, in 1993

Orchard Books, 95 Madison Avenue, New York, NY 10016

Printed and bound in Hong Kong

10 9 8 7 6 5 4 3 2 1

Library of Congress Cataloging-in-Publication Data

Chadwick, Tim.
Cabbage moon/story by Tim Chadwick: pictures by Piers Harper.—
1st American ed.
— p.—cm.
Summary: Albert the rabbit doesn't like cabbage until he finds out
what the moon is really made of.
"First published in Great Britain by ABC, All Books for Children,
in 1993"—T.p. verso.
ISBN 0-531-06827-7
[1. Rabbits—Fiction. 2. Moon—Fiction. 3. Food—Fiction.]
I. Harper, Piers, ill. II. Title.
PZ7.C3474Cab 1994
[E]—dc20 93-28952

Cabbage Moon

Story by
Tim Chadwick

Pictures by
Piers Harper

Orchard Books
New York

Albert was a very curious bunny. He was always asking questions about how things worked.

"Just eat your cabbage,
and I'll explain," his mother
would say. But Albert didn't like
cabbage and wouldn't eat it, not
for all the answers in the world.

Albert's mother didn't mind about the questions, but she did mind about the cabbage. Imagine a rabbit not liking cabbage!

But Albert was busy wondering why the sky was blue and why carrots were orange, and other important things.

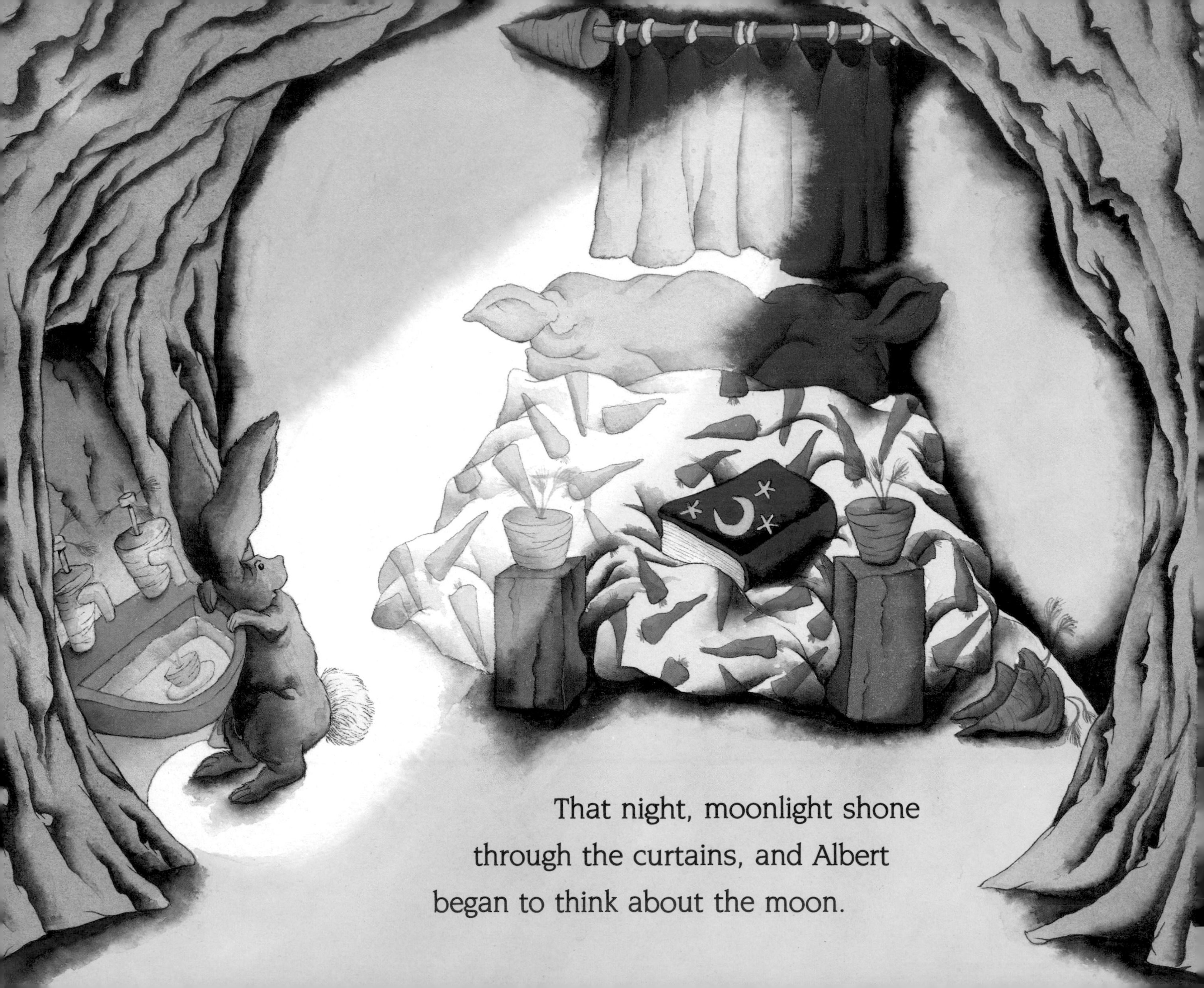

That night, moonlight shone
through the curtains, and Albert
began to think about the moon.

His parents had told him
it was made of rock and sand.
But how could something made
of rock change its shape?

Albert began to feel
as though he were floating.

Up, up he went,
through his
open window...

...past the trees
and clouds and
stars until...

...THUMP!
He landed on the moon.

Albert was surprised. The moon wasn't rock and sand. It was pale green and crisp. The moon was an enormous cabbage!

"Hey, you!" said a plump rabbit. "Follow me. We have work to do." And he lifted Albert onto a huge leaf where a group of rabbits was munching the cabbage under their feet.

"I don't like cabbage, but thank you anyway," said Albert.

"Try it," yawned Plump. "You'll be surprised."

Plump was right. This cabbage was delicious.

Albert lined up next to
the other rabbits and
began crunching.
What a feast!

Soon an enormous chunk had been eaten out of the cabbage moon and Plump began waddling around with a tape measure and stopwatch, checking and rechecking.

"Stop, please," he said. "That's all we need for tonight. Now back to your beds."

One by one, all the rabbits jumped onto the moonbeam and slid down to Earth.

But Albert was curious, and he
stayed to ask Plump some questions.

"Well," said Plump, "now you know how the full moon becomes a crescent. Simply good appetites and accurate measurement.

"In two weeks we have munched a whole cabbage moon. And because we are closer to the rain clouds and warm sun, cabbages grow much faster, so there's always a new moon when we need it."

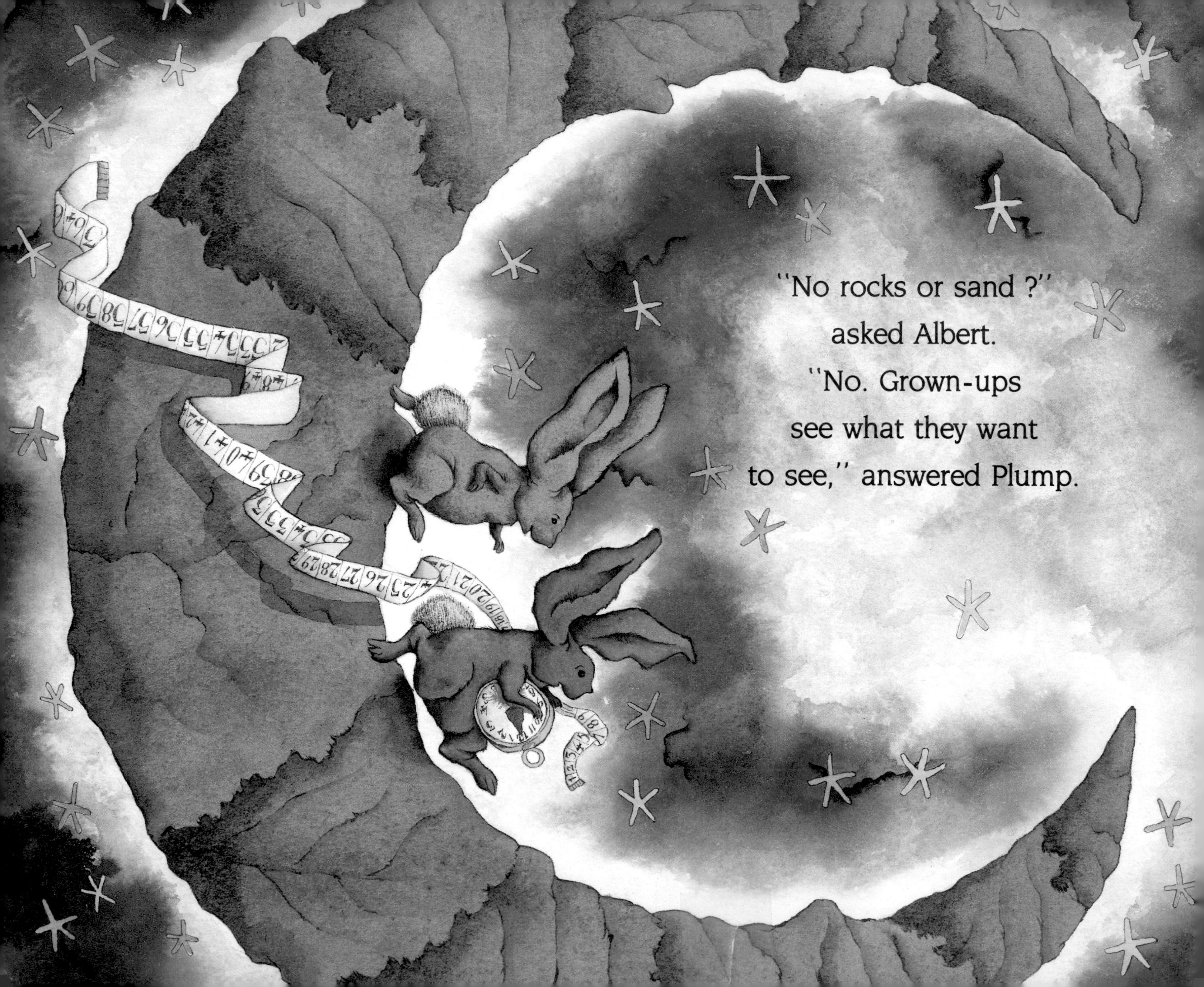

"No rocks or sand ?"
asked Albert.
"No. Grown-ups
see what they want
to see," answered Plump.

"Now jump on that moonbeam
before the sun comes up, or your
mother won't see you in your
bed and we'll be in trouble."

And Albert fell . . .

. . . and fell . . .

...and landed, snug in his bed.

That morning Albert
looked at the moon
fading into the dawn
sky. "Pretty good job,"
he said.

And it was his mother's turn
to be curious when Albert ate
every cabbage leaf on the plate —
but left the carrots.